Algoood . . . my sweet Auden and Jara Jane . . .
Sipping tea with the Moon and the Sun
Smiling, laughing . . . always watching over you.
. . . I SAW THAT ☺ —Aumma

To Yumi with respect and admiration —N.S.

Text copyright © 2020 by Yumi Heo

Jacket art and interior illustrations copyright © 2020 by Naoko Stoop

All rights reserved. Published in the United States by Schwartz & Wade Books, an imprint of Random House Children's Books, a division of Penguin Random House LLC, New York.

Schwartz & Wade Books and the colophon are trademarks of Penguin Random House LLC.

Visit us on the Web! rhcbooks.com

Educators and librarians, for a variety of teaching tools, visit us at RHTeachersLibrarians.com

Library of Congress Cataloging-in-Publication Data is available upon request.
ISBN 978-0-385-39033-0 (hc)
ISBN 978-0-385-39034-7 (lib. bdg.)
ISBN 978-0-385-39035-4 (ebook)

The text of this book is set in Graham Bold.
The illustrations were rendered in mixed media on plywood and finished digitally.
Book design by Rachael Cole
MANUFACTURED IN CHINA
1 3 5 7 9 10 8 6 4 2
First Edition

Sun and Moon have a tea party

written by **yumi heo**
illustrated by **naoko stoop**

schwartz & wade books • new york

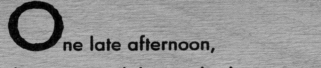

One late afternoon,
the moon and the sun had a tea party.

"Do you know," said Moon, "what moms and dads do?
They get their children ready for bed."
She took a sip of tea.

"No, they don't," said Sun.
"Moms and dads get their
children ready for school."

"Not so," said Moon. "Children have to go to sleep."

"Wrong!" replied Sun. "Children have to go to school.

"They walk down bustling sidewalks and across busy streets."

"Streets aren't busy! They are as dark and as lonely as a moonless sky,"
said Moon.

"No, no! Streets are filled with people, just like the sky is filled with birds," said Sun.

"How can birds fill the sky," said Moon, "when they are always snuggled down in their nests?"

"How can birds snuggle down," said Sun, "when they are flying over everything but us—

above rivers like mirrors and wildflowers that
bow hello in the wind?"

"Rivers can only reflect my face," said Moon.

"They can reflect mine, too," said Sun.

"I'm right, and you're wrong," said Moon, putting down her cup.

"No, *I'm* right, and *you're* wrong!" said Sun, putting down his cookie.

Just then, Cloud drifted by. "What are you two arguing about?" he asked.

And so they explained.

"Moon, you are right," said Cloud. "And, Sun, you are right too.
You must each stay up past your bedtime, and you will see."

Early the next morning, sleepy Moon rubbed her eyes and hid behind Cloud. This is what she saw:

Moms and dads pouring cereal and putting on coats, dogs chasing their tails, and trees standing guard in green uniforms.

Moon exclaimed, "How beautiful! Even the morning glories are saying good morning."

All day long the world was abuzz with activity.

As dusk fell, sleepy Sun rubbed his eyes and hid behind Cloud. This
is what he saw:

Moms and dads tucking in blankets and reading stories,
dogs sweetly dreaming, and trees standing guard in gray pajamas.

"Who would have guessed?" Sun exclaimed.

"Even the morning glories are fast asleep."

All night long the world was still.

The following day, Sun thought of Moon.

And the following night, Moon thought of Sun.

And in the world below, everything . . .

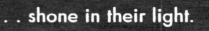

. . . shone in their light.